Dear Parents and Educators,

Welcome to Penguin Young Readers! As parents and educators, you know that each child develops at his or her own pace—in terms of speech, critical thinking, and, of course, reading. Penguin Young Readers recognizes this fact. As a result, each Penguin Young Readers book is assigned a traditional easy-to-read level (1–4) as well as a Guided Reading Level (A–P). Both of these systems will help you choose the right book for your child. Please refer to the back of each book for specific leveling information. Penguin Young Readers feature esteemed authors and illustrators, stories about favorite characters, fascinating nonfiction, and more!

Tiny Goes Back to School

LEVEL **1**

GUIDED READING LEVEL **D**

This book is perfect for an **Emergent Reader** who:
- can read in a left-to-right and top-to-bottom progression;
- can recognize some beginning and ending letter sounds;
- can use picture clues to help tell the story; and
- can understand the basic plot and sequence of simple stories.

Here are some **activities** you can do during and after reading this book:
- Character Traits: Tiny is a very different dog after he goes to school. For example, before he goes to school, he is disobedient. After he goes to school, he is obedient. Write down a list of character traits that describes Tiny *before* he goes to school, and then write a list that describes him *after* he goes to school.
- Creative Writing: Work with the child to create a poster for a dog school. What would the school teach? Where would its classes be held? How many dogs could it accommodate? Be creative and have fun!

Remember, sharing the love of reading with a child is the best gift you can give!

—Bonnie Bader, EdM
  Penguin Young Readers program

*Penguin Young Readers are leveled by independent reviewers applying the standards developed by Irene Fountas and Gay Su Pinnell in *Matching Books to Readers: Using Leveled Books in Guided Reading*, Heinemann, 1999.

For Marni and Samir and all the doggies —CM

To Jimmy M. Thank you for all the help and support you have invested in me as a working artist and as a friend! We won't forget all the stories and memories! —RD

PENGUIN YOUNG READERS
Published by the Penguin Group
Penguin Group (USA) LLC, 375 Hudson Street, New York, New York 10014, USA

USA | Canada | UK | Ireland | Australia | New Zealand | India | South Africa | China

penguin.com
A Penguin Random House Company

Text copyright © 2014 by Cari Meister. Illustrations copyright © 2014 by Richard D. Davis. All rights reserved. Published by Penguin Young Readers, an imprint of Penguin Group (USA) LLC, 345 Hudson Street, New York, New York 10014. Manufactured in China.

Library of Congress Cataloging-in-Publication Data is available.

ISBN 978-0-448-48134-0 (pbk)   10 9 8 7 6 5 4 3 2 1
ISBN 978-0-670-78607-7 (hc)   10 9 8 7 6 5 4 3 2 1

TINY Goes Back to School

by Cari Meister
illustrated by Rich Davis

Penguin Young Readers
An Imprint of Penguin Group (USA) LLC

Tiny is a good dog.

He does what I say.

4

Watch.

Sit, Tiny.

Oh no!

Shake, Tiny.

Oh no!

Stay, Tiny.

Oh no!

You need to go back to school!

Come on, Tiny.

It is okay.

There are a lot of dogs!

That makes Tiny happy.

That makes Tiny VERY happy.

No, Tiny!

Get down.

20

No, Tiny!

Come back!

The teacher comes.

He brings treats.

Now Tiny is good.

Sit, Tiny!

Shake, Tiny!

Good boy.

All the dogs want treats.

Tiny shows them what to do.

Doggie
num-nums

Sit, dogs.

Shake, dogs.

Stay, dogs.

Good dogs!

Tiny is a great teacher.